Meeting My Anxiety

By Elisa Silverglade Rader

Illustrated by Joycelyne Guerra

A Civin Media Relations Project

ISBN: 9781985300781

Printed in the United States
Kindle Direct Publishing

Project Managed by Tammi Croteau Keen
www.civinmediarelations.com
Civin Media Relations

Dedication

For my heart and soul

my beautiful boys

Joe and Jackson

--

For Jennifer Rosvally and

Tara Brach, both of whom taught

me how to meet my anxiety

--

For Disney Pixar's Inside Out

who introduced millions to the ancient

Buddhist practice of personifying emotions

anx·i·e·ty

noun

a feeling of worry, nervousness, or unease, typically about an imminent event or something with an uncertain outcome.

Her clothes

are

mismatched

and

don't

fit,

Her

outlandish appearance

and

jerky

motions

My lungs fill with breath. My chest rises.

I see her crazy hair and bright colors. I notice how loud her voice is. I wonder what she needs.

My breath goes back out through my nose...
slowly…. slowly...

My Anxiety looks so extreme that I smile,

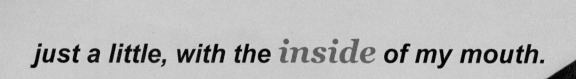

just a little, with the inside of my mouth.

I feel my body letting go...letting go.

I know what to do! *I GREET my Anxiety with a smile. I OPEN my arms and gently place my hands on her shoulders. I ASK her what she wants as I guide her to the side.*

My breath goes in through my nose.
I step forward, with curiosity,
to see
what is really happening behind my Anxiety.

My breath fills my lungs...and my belly rises.

With my Anxiety aside, I can see my capabilities.

My breath goes back out through my nose...slowly.

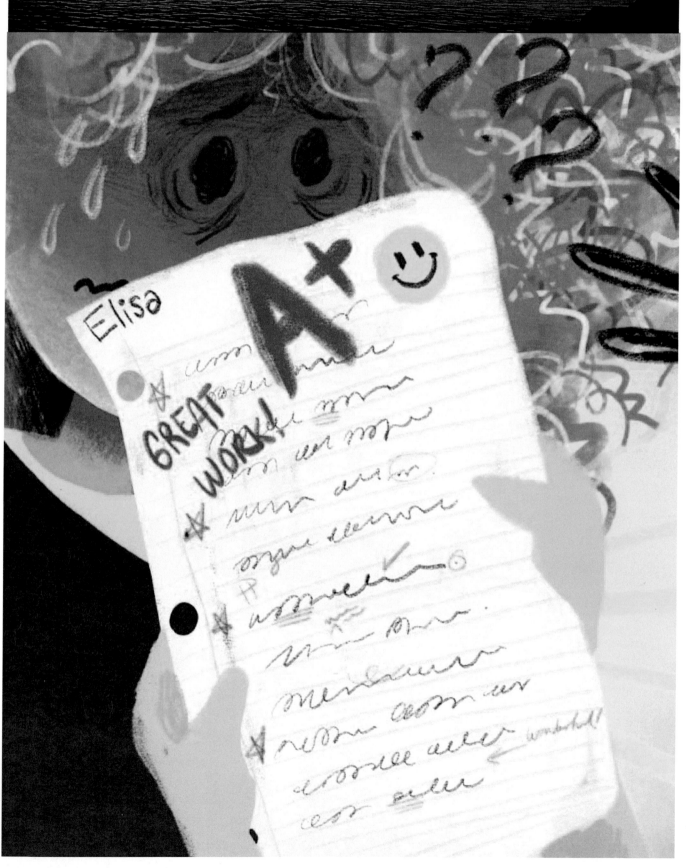

I can see my confident, knowledgeable, *STRONG* self.

My body relaxes.

I look over to my Anxiety.
I understand why she's here.
I smile and nod.
I *let* her know
I can handle things.

My belly softens...and I let go.

We **understand** each other.
Sometimes I just need to remind her
that *I am STRONG*
and *I can handle things.*

She smiles...she waves...
and with each breath I take - she fades.

My breath goes in through my nose...
and fills my lungs.
My breath goes back out through my nose...
and I let go.

About the Author
Elisa Silverglade Rader

Elisa lives in the beautiful Croton on Hudson, New York, with her two boys, Joe and Jackson. Elisa is a passionate reader, editor and sunset chaser. This is her first book.

About the Illustrator
Joycelyne Guerra

Artist Joycelyne Guerra is a recent graduate of Columbia College Chicago with a degree in Illustration. Joycelyne specializes in ink and graphite images, gouache and watercolors. She is a very versatile artist who enjoys illustrating portraits, animals, and plants. To see more of her work, visit her website, joycelyneguerra.com, or follow her on Instagram @joycelyne.guerra.

Acknowledgements

First and foremost - thank you to Todd Civin and Tammi Keen for taking on this project and especially to Tammi for her guidance, patience and constant encouragement.

I want to again thank Jennifer Rosvally for her therapy and Tara Brach for her teachings. Reading and listening to Tara began as 'homework' for Jennifer; and through both I continue to learn how to greet my anxiety with open arms, ask her what she needs and let her know I can handle anything that comes my way.

Thank you to my family - Joe and Jackson Rader, David and Terrie Silverglade, Janna, Dan, Stella and Elijah Mandell, Loni, Ethan, Jacob and Mia Roberts - for their love and their likenesses.

Special thanks to Kristin Kirkland, whose enthusiasm and appreciation for my 'poem' inspired me to pursue this project.

I'm grateful to acknowledge Spencer and Jayne Grant, Catherine Arkin, Yvette Bonnevaux, Lucy Benedetto, Chris Peske, Stacey Nusbaum, Seana O'Callaghan and Dina Kaplan - some of whom loaned their likenesses and all of whom have given me friendship, love, inspiration, encouragement and support - thank you for being on my team.

Finally, I offer my deepest, heartfelt gratitude to Joycelyne Guerra whose labor of love is the art and heart of this book.

About Crossover Yoga Project

In 2015, the Crossover Yoga Project (CYP) became a nonprofit organization with the mission to empower marginalized teen girls through trauma-informed yoga, mindfulness, and expressive arts therapy to help reduce anxiety and find their best selves.

In the past three years, CYP has met over 2,500 teen girls where they are: within residential treatment centers, runaway shelters, alternative housing and schools, detention facilities, and community programs. As they have integrated CYP's techniques into their lives, girls have reported that they are more in control of their impulses, are more self-aware of when they begin to judge themselves and others, and begin to value themselves.

When someone is affected by a traumatic experience, they develop symptoms that affect their every day judgment and behavior. CYP's curriculum was created uniquely for girls, yet the tools we share are beneficial for trauma survivors of all genders to build resilience and make positive choices.

Past participants have gained the ability to trust others and themselves, developed a sense of empathy, slept better and strengthened their capacity to focus, attributing this to academic and personal success. They report that CYP has taught them coping mechanisms that they use to confidently re-enter, connect with, and become effective community members.

CYP was founded by Elisha Simpson, ERYT, RCYT. She is a trauma survivor and is currently pursuing her second Masters in Social Work at Silberman School of Social Work at Hunter College. Her work has been featured on the digital arm of the TODAY show and the podcast Everyday Changemakers. Her husband and two amazing teenagers, Aliyah and Robbie, live in Croton-on-Hudson, NY.

For more information:

Email: info@crossoveryogaproject.org Phone: 914.319.4010

Website: www.crossoveryogaproject.org

Social Media: Facebook, Instagram, Youtube and Twitter

Everyday Changemakers - list CYP as your favorite Charity on Amazon Smile

Check out the Meeting My Anxiety Companion Activity Book available at www.civinmediarelations.com and on Amazon!

Enjoy:

   * Meeting artist Joycelyne Guerra's anxiety,

   * Coloring the pages of Meeting My Anxiety,

   * Reading real people's stories about anxiety,

   * Meditations, and

   * Other tips for managing anxiety.

Turn the page for a sneak peek!

Learn How to Meet Your GOAL with Anxiety

Greet your anxiety with

Open arms! It's just a feeling, and feelings are okay.

Ask your anxiety what it needs, why is it there?

Let your anxiety know that you can handle it!

Made in the USA
Lexington, KY
01 December 2018